Annie and Snowball and the Teacup Club

The Third Book of Their Adventures

Cynthia Rylant

Illustrated by Suçie Stevenson

SIMON & SCHUSTER BOOKS FOR YOUNG READERS

New York   London   Toronto   Sydney

For Emily Stevenson
—S. S.

SIMON & SCHUSTER BOOKS FOR YOUNG READERS
An imprint of Simon & Schuster Children's Publishing Division
1230 Avenue of the Americas, New York, New York 10020
Text copyright © 2008 by Cynthia Rylant
Illustrations copyright © 2008 by Suçie Stevenson
All rights reserved, including the right of reproduction in whole or in part in any form.
SIMON & SCHUSTER BOOKS FOR YOUNG READERS is a trademark of Simon & Schuster, Inc.
Book design by Daniel Roode
The text for this book is set in Goudy Old Style.
The illustrations for this book are rendered in pen-and-ink and watercolor.
Manufactured in the United States of America
2 4 6 8 10 9 7 5 3 1
Library of Congress Cataloging-in-Publication Data
Rylant, Cynthia.
Annie and Snowball and the Teacup Club / Cynthia Rylant ;
illustrated by Suçie Stevenson.—1st ed.
p. cm.
Summary: Annie forms a club for girls who love teacups and
other dainty things, but she will always love her
cousin Henry and his big drooly dog too.
ISBN-13: 978-1-4169-0940-8
ISBN-10: 1-4169-0940-0
[1. Tea—Fiction. 2. Clubs—Fiction. 3. Rabbits—Fiction. 4. Dogs—Fiction.
5. Cousins—Fiction.] I. Stevenson, Suçie, ill. II. Title.
PZ7.R982Ant 2008
[E]—dc22
2006039619

Contents

Teacups

Annie lived with her father
and her bunny, Snowball,
in a pretty house
with a nice front porch.

Annie liked pretty things.
Her room was full of them.
She had a frilly bed
and a frilly lamp.

She had lacy curtains
and lacy pillows.

She had little glass dogs
and little silver spoons.
And she had teacups.

Annie loved teacups.
She loved their pretty shapes
and painted flowers
and dainty little saucers.

9

Annie always wanted a
new teacup for her birthday,
and her father always gave her one.

Annie wished she knew someone
who loved teacups as much
as she did.

Her cousin Henry next door
didn't like teacups.
Henry wasn't interested in dainty things.
Henry's dog, Mudge,
weighed almost two hundred pounds,
so nothing could be dainty in
Henry's room!

Annie needed some teacup friends.
Annie needed some friends who could
be dainty.

Henry's Idea

"I need some teacup friends,"
Annie told Henry as they sat
on the front porch swing.
Mudge and Snowball were
sharing a carrot.

15

"I want to dress up
and have tea parties," Annie said.
"Yuck," said Henry.

Annie smiled.
She knew Henry would like a
mud-puddle party better.

"Maybe you can start a club,"
said Henry.
"Really?" asked Annie.
"Sure," said Henry.

Annie and Henry worked
on the sign
all afternoon.

The sign was very pretty.
It had a painted teacup,
and it read:
"A teacup club for girls.
Call Annie soon!"

Annie and Henry took the sign
to the girls' dress shop.

Mudge and Snowball came
along too.
(Snowball loved going for rides.)

After Annie and Henry put the sign up,
Annie saw a little girl and her
mother stop to read it.

"Yay!" said Annie.
"A teacup girl!"
Henry just smiled.

"You want to go play Frisbee now?"
he asked.
"Okay!" Annie said.
Annie was dainty,
but she was fun, too.

Dainty Friends

Seven little girls called Annie,
and they all loved teacups too!
Annie was very excited.

27

She asked her father to help
make club plans.
Annie and her father invited
all of the teacup girls to tea
on Saturday afternoon.

Annie's father bought
some nice cinnamon spice tea.

He helped Annie make
some sugar cookies.
(Henry and Mudge stopped by
to make sure they tasted okay.)

And Annie brought out
her very best teacups for the club.

Later the seven girls all arrived
looking like angels.
They wore flowers and bows
and lace and shiny bright shoes.

Henry saw them
from his front porch.
"They all look like Annie,"
he told Mudge.
Mudge wagged.
Mudge loved Annie.

The Teacup Club had
a wonderful time.
Some of the mothers
stayed to help.

34

Annie was proud that her dad
was such a good mother, too.
The tea was spicy and
the cookies were sugary and
the talk was all very dainty.

The Teacup Club promised
to meet once a month
at Annie's house.
Everyone was excited!

After the girls went home,
Annie went to Henry's house
to tell him all about it.
Snowball sat on Mudge's head.

"Clubs are fun!" said Annie.

"I know," said Henry. "Especially
the ones with sugar cookies."

Mudge gave Annie a big kiss.
"And maybe some drool," said Henry.

Annie laughed and hugged Mudge.
She liked dainty friends—but she
would always love her drooly
friends more!